W9-BEU-071

**north
of
everything**

north
of
everything

CRAIG CRIST-EVANS

CANDLEWICK PRESS
CAMBRIDGE, MASSACHUSETTS

Copyright © 2004 by Craig Crist-Evans

First edition 2004

Library of Congress Cataloging-in-Publication Data
Crist-Evans, Craig.
North of everything / Craig Crist-Evans. —1st. ed.
p. cm.
Summary: A family that moves from Florida to Vermont for the simpler life on a farm becomes closer to nature and each other when trials come their way. Told in free verse poems.
ISBN 0-7636-2098-X
[1. Vermont — Fiction. 2. Farm life — Vermont — Fiction. 3. Moving, Household — Fiction.] I. Title.
PZ7.C869365No 2004
[Fic] — dc22   2004045776

2   4   6   8   10   9   7   5   3

Printed in the United States of America

This book was typeset in Cushing Book.

Candlewick Press
2067 Massachusetts Avenue
Cambridge, Massachusetts 02140

visit us at www.candlewick.com

For my daughter, Kathryn

Here, north of everything,
when winter's almost done
and the sun begins to climb
above the mountains,
the old Winooski thaws.

Willows wave their pale leaves,
robins dig for worms,
and I hear the lowing cows,
           voices
                    drifting
                              soft
across the fields.

Here, north of everything,
we boil sugar from the maple trees in March,
plant long rows of corn in June, watch
October mountainsides erupt in leafy fire.

Here, north of everything,
all winter long, we sit beside the wood stove,
drinking cider, rubbing hands
to warm ourselves.

Here, north of everything,
where seasons change their clothes
from red and yellow, then white to green,
where I have learned
that fall turns to winter,
and winter turns to spring.

Before I knew about the seasons,
   we lived where nothing ever
   seemed to change
   in Florida, in Miami, where
   there were buses, trains,
   airports, malls, fast-food
   restaurants, discotheques, and bars.

The streets were jammed
   with motorcycles, trucks, and cars.

Palm trees jutted up along the sidewalks.
Just down the block, the ocean
stretched to where the sun came up.

Everything smelled like flowers.
All the time!
I only knew what snow was
from movies and picture books.

Dad worked in an office.
Mom worked at school.

Dad grew up with cows and horses,
the smells of barns and leather.

His family farmed for generations.
As far back as anyone remembers,

they worked their Pennsylvania homesteads,
then migrated westward to Ohio,

settled new farms, and fought for the Union
in the War Between the States.

His great-great-grandfather
got shot in the leg

and still came back to plow
another forty years.

I think Dad got tired
of wearing ties to work,
sitting in traffic for hours,
waiting
for a light to change.

He said good clean dirt
would make all the difference
in the world.

We bought a farm,
Dad said, his hands
in his lap, fingers
laced together.

Mom smiled
like a cat
who'd swallowed
a canary.

I sat at the dinner table,
chewing something.

There's no way
I could tell you
what it was.

We sold our house,
packed furniture and clothes,
pots and pans, my trunk of toys,
everything in stacks and stacks of boxes,

and then I wandered
through the empty rooms,
listening
to the echo
of my footsteps,

looking out the windows
at the tile roofs,
the orange trees,
and the palms.

In Florida,
everything was flat,
but
as we headed north,
the earth began
to rise and swell.

I remember
driving up the coast:
the Atlantic Ocean to the east,
Georgia and the Carolinas,
Washington, the Chesapeake,
New York City, Boston,

then west,

through New Hampshire
and, finally,
          Vermont.

Mountains big as God stood up.

Along the way,
rivers carved their names

through forests, cities,
little towns like Asheville,
Harpers Ferry, Hopkins Cove,
Bennington.

At last we drove
along the banks of the Winooski,
north on Interstate 89
to Montpelier,
the smallest state
capital in America.

Our farm:

is in Montpelier, Vermont,
almost as far as you can go
before you get to Canada.

Our farm:

fields still wet in late May,
sun low above the willow trees
that stand like tired ghosts
along the shallow, dark Winooski,
the Indian word for *onion* . . .
Onion River, oldest in the world.

Our farm:

a hundred acres
stretched like skin along the bank
of the Winooski.

Our farm:

an old oak tree,
a swing my dad strung up,

an old gray barn with corners
where I lie in piles of hay,
dreaming summer daydreams,
where I go to be alone,
where I hide when I am sad.

Our farm:

where my dad
said we'd start again,
this time closer
to the earth,
to the sky,
closer
to each other.

Our first summer,
we bought cows,
planted corn,
built fences,
painted barn walls,
cleared pastureland,
cut hay,
picked berries,
milked the cows,
made butter, cheese,

got used to living
in a place so quiet
you could hear
your heartbeat
when you lay
in bed
at night.

After school and all day Saturdays,
I helped in any way I could.

I crouched inside
old horse stalls,
scrubbed
manure and dirt
from smooth gray boards.

Together,
my dad and I fixed fences
that were falling down,
cut posts, strung wire,

then cleaned and primed
the old hand pump:

water, cold and clear—
delicious—rising
from the earth.

In the evenings,
we would sit outside
and watch the sun go down.

Sometimes we talked,
but mostly we were happy to be quiet,
tired from our work, knowing
there was more to do tomorrow.

Mom brought out cookies and hot chocolate,
sat in the porch swing,
put her arms around us both,
and we listened to the crickets
while the moon rose up
above the line of willows
down by the Winooski.

One morning,
Mom patted her belly.
She told me,
There's a baby
coming soon.

I remember
pressing my hand
against skin
tight as a drum,
hard as a stone.

Then,
as if a stone
could move,
I felt
a tiny
kick.

And
when I pressed my ear
to her round belly,

I could hear
the flutter
of a tiny
heart.

As Mom
grew big,
Dad got skinny
as a fence rail.

We laughed.

We joked that Mom
was gaining what he lost.

We joked that I
would have to carry
more of the work
so Dad could fatten up again.

I drifted between awake and sleep
until Dad finished telling stories
about his grandpa
who carved chairs from solid oak
and knew by the taste of dirt
how well his crops would grow,
about the women
who kept those old farmhouses warm,
who baked the bread,
who bore the babies,
who all died young
from so much work.

Sleep tight,
he said each night
when he was through.
Don't let the bedbugs bite.

And then the baby came,
a round-faced girl
with fuzzy hair,
a tiny nose,
and little
            bitty
                teeny
                    toes.

Mom and Dad
named her Carolyn.

I called her Spanky.

I don't know why.

Above the farm,
the stars are a million eyes,
God blinking down at me
from heaven.

The moon
floats above the fields,
above the old gray barn.

Everything
is silent
and I am
alone,
running
toward the house,
but
no matter
how hard
I run,
I cannot
find
the path
that leads up to
the door.

I sit up,
suddenly
awake,
sweating,
my heart
pounding.

Outside,
the wind
moves through
trees and whistles
underneath the eaves.

Dad sits on the edge of my bed,
  his big hand holding mine.

  I tell him
  about my dream,
  the stars
  like eyes of God,
  the moon
  like an open mouth,
  the sky so black
  it swallowed
  all the sounds.

  Then Spanky
  starts to wail
  in the other room.

  Dad gets up,
  crosses to the door,
  smiles back
  as if I understand
  he's got to go.

I'm not sure
I like this baby.

All she does
is cry.

Last night,
I heard them talking
in the other room,
their voices low,
the baby sleeping
down the hall.

You need to see a doctor,
Mom said.
It's getting serious.

The voice that was
my father
sounded
small.

Okay, he said.

And that was all.

Dad strains to lift a bale of last year's hay,
   struggles with the weight, breathes hard,
   sits down and wipes his forehead,
   stuffs his handkerchief back
   in his hip pocket,
   then tries again to lift the bale.

I move to help, but he motions me away.

I can do it, he says, grunting.

Cancer,
the doctor told my mother,
as if six letters,
a single word,
the sound of it being spoken,
could make it easier
to understand.

Water rushes
over rocks,
cuts away the muddy bank,
flowing fast toward
Lake Champlain.

A little cabin
someone built
a hundred years ago
leans inside a grove
of hemlock trees.

Mom is talking
to the minister,
who's standing
on a rock
beside the river.

He puts his hand
on her shoulder.
She hangs her head.

I throw a stone
into the water,

watch the ripples
spread into the current
racing west
along the bottom
of the valley.

Dad's in the bedroom
where it's dark and smells
of sweat and medicine.

Mom leaves the shades
closed tight till noon.

She comes out and says,
He's sleeping now,

then pours herself a drink
and sits down heavily
in Dad's big brown chair.

In a while, she is sleeping too.

*L*ife goes on.

At least that's what
the doctor says.

I try, but I can't watch
the Yankees beat the Red Sox,

can't read the stupid jokes
on the back of the cereal box,

can't listen to the kids at school
laugh about how dumb their sisters are,

can't breathe sometimes —
my chest feels like it's shrinking
or I'm sinking underneath the waves
of the ocean I remember,
down in Florida,
where Dad was okay
and nothing seemed to change.

I'm having trouble
concentrating. The room's
too hot, my head hurts,
and Cynthia, the girl behind me,
keeps poking me in the back.

Clock creeps.
Shadows shuffle.

Miss Stoner squeaks the chalk
across the blackboard.

The sound startles me alert.

You fell asleep,
Cynthia whispers.

Maybe that's why
she was poking me.

Please, God, I don't ask for much.
My dad's a good man and I love him.
Mom won't know what to do without him.

Please God,
       I don't ask for much.

In Dad's room,
sun falls through
the slanted shades,
bars of light and dark
across his frail body.

Mom boils water for tea.

On the kitchen floor,
Spanky plays with blocks,
bright-colored letters
painted on all four sides.

As I watch her play, I think,

If I could spell a prayer with all those blocks,
would God make Dad better?

After school today,
    I saw Cynthia, standing
    by the big oak tree.

    She waited till I was close and asked,
    Can I walk with you?

    Sure, I said.

    And so together,
    we walked along the rutted
    dirt road toward my house,
    kicking stones,
    and watching mist rise
    from the meadow.

    I heard about your dad,
    she said. *How is he?*

    I turned away.

    She took my hand
    and we walked the rest of the way
    without talking.

Be strong,
was all Mom said,
but I knew she meant
Get ready.

She was sewing
buttons on the shirt
Dad wore on Sundays.

Mom? I said.
*Can we go back
to Florida?*

She held the needle
motionless
for just a second,

then pushed
it through
the button.

We'll make do here,
she whispered.

And then,
cradling the shirt
as if it were a baby,
she looked at me and said,

You know
I love you,
don't you?

Spanky stood today,
  shakily,
  hands gripping the coffee table.

  Propped up on the couch, Dad watched.

  His face is thin,
  the pockets underneath
  his eyes so deep.
  It's hard to tell,
  but I think
  he almost
  smiled.

He lies so still, I don't
   know if he's still breathing,
   but his sunken chest
   lifts just a little,
   then falls again.

Mom bends over him,
rubbing his hands,
whispering,

            Please don't go.

Small, rough sounds
come from his mouth.

And then he doesn't move.
He doesn't move at all.

The doctor holds my mother
            and
she's crying
            and
she's beating on his back,
her small hands curled up in fists.

The first days
are the hardest.

Everything seems
empty. No one
smiles. Birds
keep singing, but
their songs sound sad.

Spanky swings
on the rope swing in the yard.
Mom pushes her,
but you can tell
her heart is floating
a thousand miles up,
to where she says
Dad's gone.

I don't know
where he is,
but I know what he is:

      silent as the earth,
      still as water on a windless day,
      invisible as air.

Summer squash and fat tomatoes
grow among the thick green garden leaves.

Mom bends to rows, pulling weeds,
pauses, wipes her face

with a handkerchief that belonged to Dad.
Spanky splashes in a plastic pool.

Heat bends the image of the barn
rising in waves from the baking earth.

Mom goes inside the house.
She comes back out
holding a drink.

Mom took us to the park
　　where fireworks exploded
　　like cannon in the Civil War battles
　　we're studying at school.

　　Boom
　　　　　boom
　　　　　　　　boom
　　echoed from the mountains.

Mom stood apart,
watching the display,
and I watched Spanky,
standing frozen,
head tilted back,
staring up into the sky,
eyes wide as the Atlantic.

I knelt down.
Spanky, I explained,
it's Independence Day.

　　　She didn't understand.

　　　But I do.

Up here, north of everything,
    summer comes and goes
    before you know it. Now,
    the nights are growing cool.

    The song of crickets fills the air,
    peepers peep,
    fireflies dance,
    and an old barn owl
    drifts like a shadow across the field.

    There's a quick red fox
    you can sometimes see
    moving through tall grass,
    and a shaggy moose who wanders
    out from the edge of woods at dusk.

    Soon, the peepers and crickets
    will stop their singing,
    the fox will curl up and sleep,
    the moose will disappear
    into the woods till spring,

and the owl will forget
>*who*
>>*who*
>>>*who*

he is
and drift into the trees
to sleep.

The harvest moon
hangs low in the sky.

In a few days, our neighbor Jim
will drive the tractor out to cut our hay,
rake it into long windrows,
and wait for it to dry.

To everything its season,
Dad liked to say.

The cows are fat from summer.
There is the chill of autumn in the wind.

Soon snow will fall.

This morning,
   when I stepped
   out to fetch
   a load of firewood,

   I saw
   a trail
   of prints
   in the
   first thin
   sheet
   of snow:
   a rabbit
   looking
   for something
   good
   to eat.

   The tiny
   footprints
   hopped
   from the edge
   of the field

to the heart
of the
vegetable
garden,
then
back
to the field
again.

Cynthia invited me
to a party at her house.

Other kids from school
were there, and I felt funny

when their moms and dads
came by to pick them up

and take them home. When everyone
was gone except for me, Cynthia

took me out to a shed
behind her house. She put

her finger to her lips.
Shhhh . . . be quiet, she said.

There, nestled against the wall,
was a wooden cage. Inside,

five fuzzy rabbits
curled up together.

Sometimes,
   when I look across the pasture
   where Dad and I would go
   at dusk to bring the cows
   back to the milking barn,
   my hand in his,
   our breath clouding
   in the cold air,
   big cows mooing,
   moving
   through the paddock,
   barn-smell of manure,
   hay, and leather,
   I want to cry.

   Sometimes I do.

Mom is sad again.

I try to cheer her up, you know,
tell jokes or draw her pictures,

but she just sits in Dad's old chair,
holding a glass of whiskey,
leafing through a stack
of photographs.

Come here, she says.
Remember Disney World?

She holds out
a picture of Dad
in front of that castle,
Mickey shaking his hand.

Her hand trembles.

Across the meadow, ice has formed
in the deep troughs cows have worn.
As my feet break through,
broken pieces catch sun.

Dad used to say that time is short for play
and long for getting ready. We buried him
just past the barn, where the path
leads toward the old Winooski.

The sky is dark and smells like snow.
I have to feed the cows, and so
I leave the broken mirror puddles
to freeze again, and go to work.

Bright with tinsel,
   blinking lights,
   candy canes,
   and ornaments,
   the tree Mom put up
   in the living room
   almost feels
   like Christmas.

Wrapped in colored paper
with little cards that say
        From Santa,
the gifts beneath the tree
almost feel
like Christmas.

Spanky
doesn't understand
that Dad is gone.

She's too young to know
he was her dad,
or even
what a dad is.

I suppose,
for her,
it feels
like Christmas
is supposed to feel.

Mom says
   it's harder
   during holidays.

   That's why
   she didn't
   get out of bed
   today.

   I picked up
   the bottle
   and the empty glass
   and let her sleep.

Last week,
   on a clear spring morning,
   the ice floes broke.

The Onion River
bubbled up
from its cold sleep
and rushed down
through the valley.

Pushing
up from the soft, wet ground
         —crocuses—
little trumpets
of spring.

At dawn,
on the way to school,
I saw a deer
         bending,
                  drinking
at the water's edge.

After school, Cynthia asks,
Can you come over?

I call my mom, who tells me it's okay.

We ride the bus
along dirt roads
and through a wood
that stretches
all the way
to the top
of a mountain.

When we come
to her house,
I am surprised
at how the willow
in her front yard
has turned green with leaves,
how yellow daffodils
fill the beds along the walk.

Wait till you see,
she says excitedly,
and takes my hand again.

We go back to the cage
and look inside.

The five big rabbits
look out at us,
their long ears twitching.

When I look closer, I see
six new babies
curled up at the back of the cage,
sleeping in a nest of hay.

Again
the minister stands
on a rock
by the river,
like a prophet
in the Bible.

Across the pasture,
the cows are grazing
in the thick spring grass,
chewing, flicking
black flies with their tails.

The minister says something.

Mom's shoulders slump;
she hangs her head,
then takes his hand.

Just a whisper
carried to me on the wind,
her voice:

I can do it,
she says.
I know I can.

In the kitchen,
I watched Mom
fill a glass
with whiskey,
hold it
for a long time
in her hands,
then empty it
down
the drain.

I am in the tack room
with Mom and Spanky.
The smell of oiled leather
fills the room.

Mom says
Dad's spirit lives
in every blade of grass,
in every tree, in all the ways
we learn to keep on breathing.

She lifts the baby in the air.
I lean against the baled hay,
whittling on a stick of hickory.
Spanky's laughter
echoes through the barn.

Today,
Mom and Spanky and I
went to town for ice cream,

and Mom laughed
when a man
made a hat
from red balloons
and placed it
with great ceremony
on her head.

Sometimes, he said,
you just need a hat.

The air is alive
  with peepers and birds.

  You can smell the dirt.

  Bees are busy
  in the meadows.

  The cow's bellies are fat with calves.

  They walk
  slow and sway
  from side to side.

Rosco birthed her calf this morning,
a raw-boned little heifer
with wobbly newborn feet
and eyes like milky moons.

Mom came out to help.
She rolled up her sleeves,
and reached
until she pulled the baby cow
into the morning sun.

Spanky laughed,
throwing handfuls of hay
in all directions.

Cynthia had come over
to help my mom bake cookies.
When she saw the calf,
she stood there
with her mouth wide open.

I found myself
whistling a tune

I remember Dad
whistling too,
but not as good
as he could.

I drove the tractor today
for the first time ever.

It felt funny
to sit there in the seat
where Dad sat—

plowing, cutting, harvesting—

looking out across the fields, knowing
that by the end of summer,
what I planted would come in.

It's hard to keep the wheels
steady in the furrows
between the rows of corn.

But I did.

Spanky said her first word
while we were eating dinner tonight.

Dad, she said. *Dad.*

Mom stopped chewing.
So did I.

Spanky looked at both of us,
a little smile curling
at the corners of her mouth.

Dad, she said. *Dad.*

Mom reached across the table
and patted Spanky's head.

And then we went on eating.

What else could we do?

acknowledgments

Special thanks to my parents, Jim and Barb Evans, who raised me in the North then gave me the South, opening me to a nomadic life that brought me years later to New England. Thanks also to my friends in Vermont who helped me know the landscape and the culture: Bonnie Christensen, Greg Dunkling, Victor Ehly, Linda Ormsbee (whose homestead served as my model for the one in this book), Katherine Paterson, Alice Soule-Collins, Donna Stone, and Roger Weingarten. Finally, thanks always to Christine Belleris, Ashley Bryan, David Daboll, Rebecca Dotlich, Jeff Evans, Debbie and Gary Hoover, Lee Bennett Hopkins, David Patterson, Anita Silvey, and Heidi Stemple — for being brothers, sisters, and friends in life and art. And finally, thanks and deep appreciation to Linda Pratt for her tireless patience and devotion, and to Kara LaReau for her keen eye, her musical ear, and her extraordinary heart.